Spike

Written by Phil Cummings
Illustrated by David Cox

An easy-to-read SOLO
for beginning readers

SOLOS

Southwood Books Limited
3-5 Islington High Street
London N1 9LQ

First published in Australia by Omnibus Books 2001

Published in the UK under licence from
Omnibus Books by
Southwood Books Limited, 2003

ISBN 1 903207 73 8

Printed in China

A CIP catalogue record for this book is available
from the British Library

For my friends at
Salisbury Heights Primary School – P.C.

For Bridie Murphy – D.C.

Chapter 1

Every morning Joe and Spike went walking.

Joe liked to get his morning paper.

Spike liked to meet other dogs and sniff things along the way.

One morning, while he was sniffing, Spike met a cat.

Miaooww!

Spike barked.

He jumped.

He sprang and twisted on his leash.

Joe tried to hold on, but Spike was too strong for him. With a spin and a twist, he slipped out of his collar.

Off down the street he ran. *Ruff! Ruff! Ruff!* He had little legs, but he could run very fast.

Chapter 2

Joe dropped his walking stick. His glasses fell from his nose. He couldn't see very well.

"Spike! Spike!" he called.

Spike couldn't hear Joe. *Ruff!*
he went. *Ruff! Ruff!*

Spike ran after the cat.
He ran around one corner ...

and then another.
He ran over one bin ...

and then another.

He ran through a thick bush …

under a
gate …

along a path.

He ran as fast as he could, but he didn't catch the cat. It jumped on to a high wall.

Spike barked, but the cat just licked its paws.

Spike gave up. It was time to go home to Joe.

He turned to walk home, but then he stopped.

The shop had gone.

Joe had gone.

The street he knew so well had gone.

He trotted up and down streets.

He looked down alleys.

He sniffed posts.

He sniffed
flowers.

He sniffed trees.
There were no smells
he knew anywhere.

It was growing dark.
Spike was lost.

Chapter 3

Spike was hungry. He was cold, too. He couldn't stop shivering.

Under a bridge in a park he found a spot where the grass was soft and tall.

He made a bed. He tucked his head between his paws.

There were sounds in the dark. Spike couldn't sleep.

Back home, Joe couldn't sleep
either. He sat in his chair by the fire
and worried.

Where was Spike? Was he safe?

Joe fell asleep in his chair. The
TV went *fuzzzz*, but Joe didn't
wake up.

In the morning Joe put on his coat and his hat and his scarf.

He took his walking stick and walked slowly to the shop.

He looked up and down the street, and into alleys.

He got his newspaper and stood outside the shop.

People came with their dogs. Joe patted them all.

But Spike didn't come.

Chapter 4

Spike woke up in the park.

Some ducks were looking down at him.

Spike barked bravely. *Ruff! Ruff! Ruff!*

The ducks flapped away.

All around the park were busy streets. There were cars, buses and trucks everywhere.

Spike had never crossed a street by himself before. He waited for the cars to stop, but they didn't.

Spike decided to run across the
street.
Suddenly he heard the sound of
screeching tyres.

Spike was very afraid.

He stopped running.

He lay down in the middle of the road and shook with fright.

Mr Cook stopped his car just in time.

He told his children, Gabby and Jake, to wait in the car.

Mr Cook could see that the little dog wasn't hurt. He picked it up and carried it to the car.

Spike licked Gabby and Jake all over when he got in the car. They laughed.

Gabby had a ball. Spike liked to chase a ball. He and the children played with it on the seat all the way home.

Today Gabby and Jake and their parents were moving to a new house. It had a big yard.

"Can we have a dog in our new house, Dad?" Jake asked.

"Maybe," said Mr Cook. "But not this dog. He belongs to someone else."

Gabby hugged Spike. "I wonder what his name is?" she said.

Spike licked her cheek.

"I wonder who he belongs to?" said Jake.

"We'll take him to the dog pound when we've finished packing," said Mr Cook.

All day the family was busy packing. Their front garden was full of boxes, trunks and cases. The removal van was coming at three o'clock.

Gabby and Jake played with the little dog.

They threw a ball for him. He jumped and caught it.

The children clapped.

Chapter 5

At last the van came. It took a long time to load everything.

"It's too late to take the dog to the pound now," said Mr Cook. "He can come in the car with us."

The children were happy. But the little dog looked sad. He sat in the car and didn't want to play. He was thinking about Joe.

The family arrived first at the new house.

Next came the van.

Everyone was very busy.

Gabby and Jake left the little dog in the car. They thought he would be safer there.

Chapter 6

Joe put on his glasses. He looked up at the clock. There was a lot of noise outside.

"I wonder what's going on?" he thought.

Joe took his walking stick and went to look. It was nearly dark.

A huge van was parked next door.

In front of the van was a car. A man was getting something out of the boot.

Joe looked at the car. In the window he saw a face.

It was a dog's face.

It was Spike's face!

"You found my Spike!" cried Joe.
"We did?" said Mr Cook.

Joe opened the car door.

Spike jumped out.

Joe smiled. "Welcome home," he said.

"So this is *your* dog," said Mr Cook.

"Yes, it is," said Joe. "I lost him yesterday."

"We found him today," said Jake.

"Amazing!" said Mrs Cook.

Chapter 7

The new neighbours got on very well.

Mr Cook made a dog door in the fence.

Spike loved it!

Joe made a new collar for Spike.
It had his name and address on it.
"He won't get lost now," said Joe.

Just then a cat ran past.

Ruff! Ruff! Ruff!
Miaooww ...

"Oh no, not again!" said Joe.

Phil Cummings

One night, as we drove home along a dark road, we nearly hit a small dog. He seemed to be lost. As soon as we opened the car door he jumped in. We decided to keep him for the night and then try to find his home. Misty, our dog, didn't like him much. He took her spot by the heater!

We had just moved into a new house. We found out that the little dog, Spike, lived at the end of our street.

Now, when we take Misty for her walks, she is quite happy to see Spike, just as long as he stays home!

David Cox

I'm glad Phil wrote this story. I have a feeling that he likes dogs. I like dogs too, and I like drawing them. I am sort of small and furry, like Spike, so I was able to use myself as a model.

For a long time, one of my grandchildren thought I was a dog. She even called me "Pup" until she grew to about three years old.

I am getting a bit old, too, so I found Joe easy to draw. All I had to do was look in the mirror!

I enjoyed doing the illustrations for this story. Thanks, Phil.

More Solos!

Duck Down
Janeen Brian and Michael Johnson

The Monster Fish
Colin Theale and Craig Smith

The Sea Dog
Penny Matthews and Andrew Mclean

Elephant's Lunch
Kate Darling and Mitch Kane

Hot Stuff
Margaret Clark and Tom Jellett

Spike
Phil Cummings and David Cox

Lily and the Wiazrd Wackoo
Judy Fitzpatrick and Don Hatcher

Sticky Stuff
Kate Walker and Craig Smith